T0365609

Jeepney Love ♥
A Children's Story

Written by
Winifred "Oyoko" Loving

Illustrated by
Vince Raphael Clorina

Order this book online at www.trafford.com
or email orders@trafford.com

Most Trafford titles are also available at major online book retailers.

Print information available on the last page.

ISBN: 978-1-4907-7248-6 (sc)
      978-1-4907-7249-3 (e)

Library of Congress Control Number: 2016905824

Our mission is to efficiently provide the world's finest, most comprehensive book publishing
service, enabling every author to experience success. To find out how to publish your book,
your way, and have it available worldwide, visit us online at www.trafford.com

Any people depicted in stock imagery provided by Thinkstock are models,
and such images are being used for illustrative purposes only.
Certain stock imagery © Thinkstock.

Trafford rev. 04/15/2016

www.trafford.com
North America & international
toll-free: 1 888 232 4444 (USA & Canada)
fax: 812 355 4082

Dedication

Jeepneys are the most popular means of transportation in the Philippines. As you walk the streets of Manila, it is quite impossible not to hear its loud and distinct sounds. Oh I remember my first jeepney ride. Shaking and nervous like the little boy I was, I mustered my courage and entered the jeepney.

Before someone enters a jeepney, many fascinating elements will attract your attention. The metal sculptures, the colorful signages, and most of all, the different artworks that lie on both sides of the vehicle. Jeepneys provide an avenue for people, young and old, to realize that art can be expressed in many ways.

As the passengers quickly fill up the vehicle, I experienced different things. The knees of the passengers are so close to each other that it gets quite uncomfortable. Someone would suddenly ask you to pass their fare to the driver. "Pasuyo", they would say. The drivers enthralled me for they really know how to multitask. Driving in Manila is enough to pour all your focus on, but try adding the computing of fares and of course, the alertness when the driver hears the word " Para!". "Para" means to move aside in Filipino. It is the common term we use to tell the driver that we are about to alight from the jeepney.

May this book serve as a vibrant memory of Mommy Winnie's first visit to the Pearl of the Orient: The Philippines. The time may have been short, but as you look through the pages, I hope you think of the sights and sounds Manila instilled in you. Thank you for making me a part of this wonderful book.

Vince Raphael P. Clorina

The roads were full of cars and vans that early day in downtown Manila Bay.

The tricycles were speeding and leading the way! Motorcycles blasted past!
The jeepneys were jammed, full of people going to work.

4

Children in their uniforms were hurrying to school. Bicycles were buzzing by...oh my!

The buses were crowded, crammed, and creaking.
Their brakes and engines were squeaking.
Inside the jeepneys, their passengers were reading,
checking their phones, ready to go.

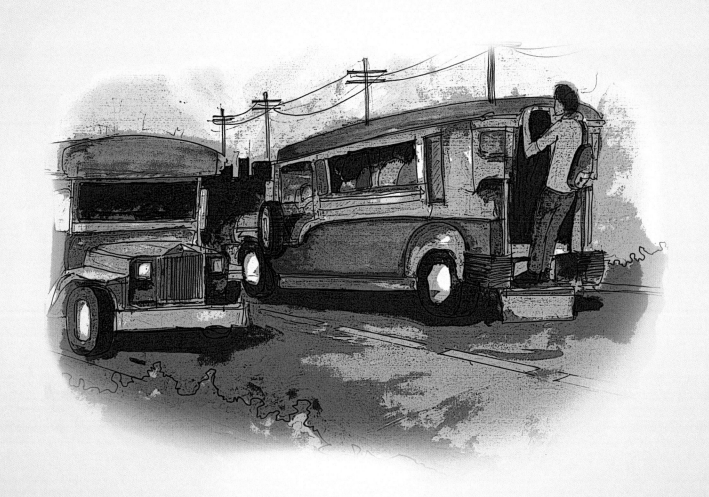

Quite suddenly, out of the blue, two brightly colored jeepneys nearly collided on the corner by the statue of Jose Rizal.

10

"HEY!", he said with a sad face. "HEY!", said she with a mad face.
"I'm so sorry," he sputtered.
"Watch where you are going," she fumed.

They bustled through the traffic, onto the long highways, and down tiny streets. Near the museum, around the parks, and over the bridges they went.

14

The buyers and sellers in the markets were busy, busy, busy,
shaded by a rainbow of bright, sunny umbrellas,
and smiling as the jeepneys hurried by.

16

The little jeepneys were tired, tired, tired at the end of the day... busted, dusty, and thirsty.

They both drove into, surprisingly, the same gas station before going home.
"Oh no, not you again," she said, blushing with a small smile.
"I remember you!", he chugged hopefully as he parked.

"So, what's your name?", he asked, wiping his windows.
"Loving Kindness*", she chirped. "And yours?"
"Tender Mercies*", he revved smoothly.

They both laughed, coughed a little, and then laughed some more. "Well, I guess we were meant to be together." they both said with joy.

About the Author

A Bostonian by birth, Winifred Marie Loving received her Bachelor of Arts degree from Newton College of the Sacred Heart and her Masters of Science in Education from Wheelock College. She has travelled the world to many islands, far-flung countries, and all the fifty states. (Her favorite state is Hawaii.) While travelling in Ghana, she received the pen-name "Oyoko" which means "member of the royal clan." She moved to the Caribbean years ago...and has been living there happily ever after. She taught elementary school for thirty years while raising a family, a daughter and a son who also work in the teaching profession. Mrs. Loving is an avid reader, an intrepid traveler, and a fan of gospel music. Her husband is a sailor and builder of model boats. She has published two books of poetry, Remember When and Spontaneous. Her first children story, My Name is Freedom, is available at www.trafford.com and www.amazon.com. She would love to write another book while travelling through the south of France. You can contact Winifred directly at oyoko_vi@yahoo.com. It's story time!

25

About the Illustrator

Vince Raphael Clorina is an Architecture student studying at the University of Sto. Tomas, Manila, Philippines. He currently resides in Bacoor City, Cavite and lives happily with his family. With a passion for art and music, he uses these to keep himself delighted and occupied.

Jeepney Love ♥

Printed in the United States
by Baker & Taylor Publisher Services